The Berenstain Bears
and
TOO MUCH
CAR TRIP

Never take cubs on long drives
is a pretty good tip.
But there may come a time
when it's all worth the trip.

The Berenstain Bears
and
TOO MUCH
CAR TRIP

Stan & Jan Berenstain

HarperFestival®
A Division of HarperCollins*Publishers*

It was just about vacation time for the Bear Family.
Brother and Sister Bear knew where *they* wanted to go on
vacation. Brother's choice was Great Grizzlyland. "Cousin
Fred's been there twice," he said. "He says it has all the
biggest, steepest, fastest rides!"

Sister had a different idea. She wanted to go to Wild
White Water Kingdom. "Lizzy went there last year and she
says it's awesome! It's got a white water ride where everybody
has to wear a bathing suit. It's got a pool that makes
a huge wave, a corkscrew waterslide and . . . "

"I'm sure those places are fun," interrupted Papa Bear, "but we're going on a different sort of vacation this year."

"Oh?" said Brother. "Where are we going?"

"We're going on a car trip," said Papa. "As a matter of fact, I'm planning it right now on this road map." He was seated at the dining room table. He had a big map spread out on it.

"A car trip?" said the cubs. That's what the cubs
said. But that's not what they were thinking. What
they were thinking was: *Oh no, not a car trip! Not
a long, boring car trip!*

"A car trip to where?" asked Brother.

"Your mother and I have decided that it's time
for you two to see more of the country," said Papa.

Sister was puzzled. "What country is that?" she
asked.

Papa looked up from the map. "Why, Bear Country, of course," he said.

"What kind of vacation is that?" asked Brother. "We can see Bear Country any old time."

"Yeah," said Sister. "We can just look out the window."

"Besides," said Brother, "what's there to see?"

"There's a great deal to see," said Papa. "And a great deal more to appreciate. So why don't you just sit there beside me and I'll show you where we're going on this map." They climbed up on chairs beside Papa and looked at the map.

It didn't look like much of a vacation to the cubs. It looked like just what it was—a big, boring map.

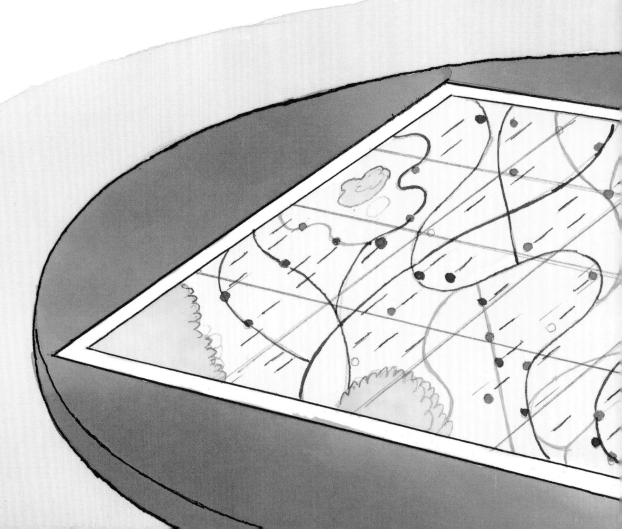

"Well, what do you two think of our vacation plans?" asked Mama Bear, coming into the room with baby Honey.

"Is Honey coming with us on this car trip?" asked Sister.

"Goodness no," said Mama. "She's not old enough to appreciate a trip like this. I've arranged for Honey to stay with Gramps and Gran while we're away."

Lucky Honey! thought the cubs. *She gets to have fun with Gramps and Gran while we have to go on a long, boring car trip.*

"You know," said Brother, "baby Honey is a lot of work. Why don't we stay and help Gramps and Gran while you two go on the car trip?"

Mama and Papa didn't think that was such a good idea.

They packed up and left early the next morning. After saying their good-byes to baby Honey, Gramps, and Gran, they headed for the open road.

Mama knew how the cubs felt, so she brought along things for them to do during the trip. She brought crayons, a book of mazes, and some board games. But the cubs were so determined to be bored that they ignored the things Mama had brought. They just sat in the back of the car with their arms folded.

Since they were looking straight ahead, the cubs didn't notice that the country around them was changing. The trees were getting bigger and wilder. The land was getting craggier. They didn't even notice the wide blue sky filled with great white clouds sailing and scudding over the broad country.

But there was something they did notice—a distant roaring sound. It's hard to stay bored when there's a distant roaring sound that's getting louder and louder. "What's that roaring sound?" asked Brother.

"That's Honeymoon Falls," said Mama. "It's where Papa and I spent our honeymoon."

Just then they turned a corner and there it was. Tons of water were pouring over a cliff and crashing into the river below.

Brother and Sister forgot all about being bored and said, "Wow!" They parked the car and went to Honeymoon Point overlooking the falls.
They had to rent slickers to keep from getting drenched. "*I BET THEY DON'T HAVE ANYTHING LIKE THIS AT WILD WHITE WATER KINGDOM!*" shouted Sister over the roar.

"There's something I don't quite understand, Mama," she added as they headed back to the car. "If you were here on your honeymoon, how come I don't remember it?" Mama and Papa just looked at each other as Brother whispered, "We weren't even born yet, silly!"

That gave Sister something to think about on the next leg of their car trip.

"Hey, look!" shouted Brother. "Soldiers fighting! They're shooting at each other!"

"Nothing to worry about, Son," said Papa. "They're just shooting blanks. They're reenactors."

"Huh? What's reenactors?" asked Brother.

"They're folks that act out important things that happened a long time ago."

"What are they *re-en-act-ing*?" asked Sister.

Papa looked at the map. "Hmm. I'd say it's the Battle of Beadle Creek. See that stream? That's Beadle Creek."

"Who was doing the fighting?" asked Brother.

"Folks just like us," said Papa.

"What were they fighting about?" asked Sister.

"You know, countries don't just happen," said Papa. "Folks have to make them happen. And sometimes there's trouble. That's what the reenactors want us to think about. Sometimes you can learn from the past and do a better job in the future. Look over there, behind that low wall."

The cubs looked.

"See those stones?" asked Papa.
"They mark the graves of the
soldiers who fell in battle."
    Brother started to say "Wow!"
but nothing came out. Sister took
hold of Mama's hand and leaned
against her.

Back on the road they went up, up, uphill for a long time. They passed a sign that said ELEVATION 7,610 FT.

"What's that sign mean?" asked Brother.

"We're in the Great Grizzly Mountains and that's how high we are," said Mama.

That's when they turned a corner and
found themselves looking down the
steepest, narrowest, windingest road
they had ever seen. The wind rushed
past as they plunged down the mountain.

"Whew!" said Brother when they got to
the bottom. "I bet they don't have anything
like that at Great Grizzlyland."

"That's a pretty safe bet," said Papa.

They passed a sign that said NOW ENTERING BEAR COUNTRY NATIONAL PARK: HOME OF MOUNT GRIZZMORE. "What's a national park, Mama?" asked Sister.

"It's a park that belongs to the whole country," said Mama.

"What's Mount Grizzmore?" asked Brother.

"It's a very special mountain," said Papa.

"What's special about it?" asked Sister.

"You'll see in a minute, dear," said Mama.

Mount Grizzmore came into view as they came out of a clump of trees. And it really *was* special. It had three enormous faces carved in its side.

"Who are they?" asked Brother from the observation area.

"They're some of the great heroes of Bear Country history," said Papa. "Their faces are carved in the mountain so we won't forget them."

Brother and Sister looked up at the great faces.

A picture came into Brother Bear's mind's eye. It showed the three historic faces, but there was another one, too.

It was the face of Brother Bear. "A penny for your thoughts, Son," said Papa.

"Er, uh . . . I was just thinking how this trip is a lot different from what I expected," he said.

Of course, there was a lot more that happened during the Bear family's car trip.

There were spilled drinks,

bathroom stops (lots),

sticky lollipops,

souvenir stops,

motel stops,

and all the other things that usually go with
car trips. But that's not what the cubs remembered.
What they remembered was the big sky,
the great falls, the mighty mountains, the little
graveyard at Beadle Creek, and the heroes of
Bear Country's history in the side of a mountain.

Baby Honey Bear was asleep when they picked her up at Gramps and Gran's and headed home. "You know something, Papa," said Brother as they climbed the steps of the tree house. "We ought to take Honey on a car trip sometime—when she's old enough to appreciate it, of course."

"Of course," said Papa.